I'm a
Ballerina!

By Sue Fliess
Illustrated by Joey Chou

A GOLDEN BOOK · NEW YORK

Text copyright © 2015 by Sue Fliess
Illustrations copyright © 2015 by Joey Chou
All rights reserved. Published in the United States by Golden Books, an imprint of Random House
Children's Books, a division of Penguin Random House LLC, 1745 Broadway, New York, NY 10019, and
in Canada by Random House of Canada, a division of Penguin Random House Ltd., Toronto. Golden Books,
A Golden Book, A Little Golden Book, the G colophon, and the distinctive gold spine are
registered trademarks of Penguin Random House LLC.
randomhousekids.com
Educators and librarians, for a variety of teaching tools, visit us at
RHTeachersLibrarians.com
Library of Congress Control Number: 2014943497
ISBN 978-0-553-49758-8 (trade) — ISBN 978-0-553-49759-5 (ebook)
Printed in the United States of America
20 19 18 17 16 15 14 13
Random House Children's Books supports the First Amendment and celebrates the right to read.

*B*allet lessons! Time to go—
We head for the studio!

First we balance on the barre,
Leaning over, reaching far,

Stretching arms and legs out long.
Ballet dancers must be strong!

Five positions in ballet—

second position

first position

We'll review them
all today!

third position

fourth position

fifth position

Next we plié and chassé,
Pirouette, petit jeté.

We've been working hard all year.
Our recital's finally here!

Last rehearsal for the show—
Get it right from

head

to

toe.

Twist my hair up in a bun—
Getting dressed is half the fun!
Tutu, tights, a crown, some bows . . .

Mom puts powder on my nose.
Ballet slippers for my feet.
Now my costume is complete!

My recital starts at eight.
"Hurry up! We can't be late!"

The music is about to start!
"What if I forget my part?"
"Take some deep breaths.
    You'll be great!"
I breathe in and
    stand up straight.

Fix my tutu. Tug my tights.
My instructor dims the lights.

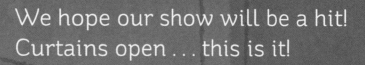

We hope our show will be a hit!
Curtains open ... this is it!

That's my number.
Here I go. . . .
I can't believe
I'm in a show!

Gracefully we bend and rise,
Arms like wings of butterflies.

Perfectly I pirouette!
But the show's not over yet....

Glide and twirl, leap . . . and land.
All the parents clap and stand!

Time for me to take a bow.
I'm a ballerina now!